Sunny Sunday Drive

Editor: Jill Kalz
Page Production: Tracy Kaehler
Creative Director: Keith Griffin
Editorial Director: Carol Jones

First American edition published in 2006 by
Picture Window Books
5115 Excelsior Boulevard
Suite 232
Minneapolis, MN 55416
877-845-8392
www.picturewindowbooks.com

First published in Australia by
Ice Water Press
An imprint of @Source Pty Limited
Unit 3, Level 1, 114 Old Pittwater Road
Brookvale NSW 2100 Australia
Ph: 61 2 9939 8222; Fax: 61 2 99398666
Email: sales@sourceoz.com
Copyright © 2004 by Ice Water Press

Printed in the United States of America.

Library of Congress Cataloging-in-Publication Data
Scott, Janine.
Sunny Sunday drive / by Janine Scott ; illustrated by Ian Forss.
p. cm. — (Farmer Claude and Farmer Maude)
Summary: When Farmer Claude and Farmer Maude go for a drive with
their animals, the people in the cab and the animals in the back of the truck
have entirely different opinions about the weather and the pleasure of the trip.
ISBN 1-4048-1696-8 (hardcover)
[1. Weather—Fiction. 2. Automobile travel—Fiction. 3. Farmers—Fiction.
4. Domestic animals—Fiction. 5. Stories in rhyme.] I. Forss, Ian, ill. II. Title.
PZ8.3.S4275Sun 2005
[E]—dc22   2005029439

Farmer Claude and Farmer Maude

Sunny Sunday Drive

by Janine Scott

illustrated by Ian Forss

PICTURE WINDOW BOOKS
Minneapolis, Minnesota

Farmer Claude and Farmer Maude
went for a Sunday drive.
Farmer Claude and Farmer Maude
sat in the front of the truck.

A female chicken is called a hen. A group of hens is called a brood.

The dog, the goat, the rooster, and the pig came on their Sunday drive.
The dog, the goat, the rooster, and the pig sat in the back of the truck.

"Which way should we go?"
cried Farmer Claude.

"Follow the sun!"
cried Farmer Maude.

The sun always rises in the east. It always sets in the west.

They drove their truck up the hills

and down the hills

and along the sunny road.

Farmer Claude and Farmer Maude
went thumpity-jumpity-bump.

The dog, the goat, the rooster, and the pig went humpity-lumpity-clump.

When a dog is worried, the hair along its neck and spine stands up.

Farmer Claude and Farmer Maude didn't look left and didn't look right. Farmer Claude and Farmer Maude looked at the road ahead.

"Why don't you look behind you?"
the shaken animals said.

A large, dark cloud is
called a thunderhead.
It usually carries a lot
of rain.

But Farmer Claude and Farmer Maude
couldn't hear the animals say:
"Rain, rain, go away.
Come again another day!"

Farmer Claude and Farmer Maude
didn't look left and didn't look right.
Farmer Claude and Farmer Maude
looked at the road ahead.

"Why don't you look behind you?"
the shivering animals said.

When you are cold, you shake, or shiver. Shivering is your body's way of trying to warm up.

But Farmer Claude and Farmer Maude couldn't hear the animals say:
"Wind, wind, go away.
Come again another day!"

A strong wind is called a gale. Tree branches may break off in a gale.

Farmer Claude and Farmer Maude
looked at the sky ahead.
"This is a perfect Sunday drive.
It is just right," they said.

The dog, the goat, the rooster, and the pig
looked at the sky behind.
"This is an awful Sunday drive.
It is a fright," they whined.

Then Farmer Claude and Farmer Maude
turned back with their load.
Down the hills and up the hills
and along the sunny road.

"That sunny Sunday drive was fun," they said. "We're lucky it was fine."

The animals just drooped and dripped
and then began to whine.
"That sunny Sunday drive," they said,
"was very far from FINE!"

1. What day did Farmer Claude and Farmer Maude go on their drive?

2. Name the four animals that rode in the back of the truck.

3. What was Farmer Maude's answer when Farmer Claude asked, "Which way should we go?"

4. Who looked at the road ahead? And who looked at the road behind?

5. What kinds of weather did the animals feel in the back of the truck?

6. What did the animals do when they got back home?

28

Rooster's Recap

ANSWERS

1. Sunday (page 4)

2. the dog, the goat, the rooster, and the pig (page 6)

3. "Follow the sun!" (page 9)

4. Farmer Claude and Farmer Maude looked at the road ahead; the animals looked behind (pages 14 and 15)

5. rain and wind (pages 16 and 20)

6. drooped, dripped, and began to whine (page 26)

To Learn More

On the Web

FactHound offers a safe, fun way to find Internet sites related to this book. All of the sites on FactHound have been researched by our staff.

1. Visit *www.facthound.com*
2. Type in this special code for age-appropriate sites: 1404816968
3. Click on the FETCH IT button.

Your trusty FactHound will fetch the best sites for you!

At the Library

DK Publishing. *Farm Animals*. New York: DK Publishing, 2004.

Kutner, Merrily. *Down on the Farm*. New York: Holiday House, 2004.

Murphy, Andy. *Out and About at the Dairy Farm*. Minneapolis: Picture Window Books, 2004.

Wolfman, Judy. *Life on a Dairy Farm*. Minneapolis: Carolrhoda Books, 2004.

READY FOR MORE ADVENTURES?

Charming and funny, Farmer Claude and Farmer Maude are anything but boring. Full of great ideas and in love with adventure, these odd farmers know how to have a good time wherever they are!

Farmer Claude

Farmer Maude

Pig

Goat

Rooster

Dog

What a group of unlucky characters! Storm clouds follow them, rain soaks their beds, and the farmers wake them at the crack of dawn. But the animals make it through together—and even share a smile or two.

Look for All of the Books in the Farmer Claude and Farmer Maude Series: